THE STORY OF HANUMAN

Mala Dayal has been involved with developing, editing and writing material for children for over forty years. She is the author of *Nanak: The Guru, The Ramayana in Pictures* and *The Story of Krishna*, all published by Rupa.

Taposhi Ghoshal is an illustrator and graphic designer. She spent her early professional years with the NGO, Katha, and has worked as a freelance illustrator since 1993. She has illustrated and designed several children's books and magazines for leading publishing houses. She was the Indian nominee for the International Board on Books for Young People (IBBY) Honourlist 2008 for her illustrations in the picture book, *Panna*.

THE STORY OF
HANUMAN

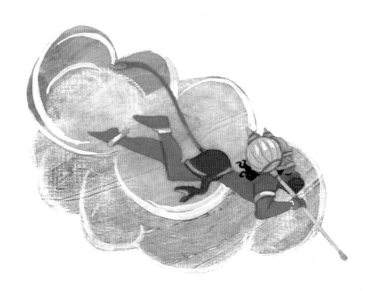

text by
Mala Dayal & Taposhi Ghoshal
illustrated by

RED TURTLE
RUPA

Published in Red Turtle by
Rupa Publications India Pvt. Ltd 2016
7/16, Ansari Road, Daryaganj
New Delhi 110002

Sales centres:
Allahabad Bengaluru Chennai
Hyderabad Jaipur Kathmandu
Kolkata Mumbai

ISBN: 978-81-291-3717-3
First impression 2016

10 9 8 7 6 5 4 3 2 1

The moral right of the author has been asserted.

Printed at Lustra Print Process Pvt. Ltd., New Delhi

For Naina,
guardian angel,
protector

—Mala Dayal

To my school art teacher, Manab sir,
with love

—Taposhi Ghoshal

This is HANUMAN. Son of Vayu, the Wind God, and Anjana.

Hanuman could never be still. He played with large stones and shook big trees.

One day, hungry, he saw Surya, the sun, rising. He thought Surya was a fruit, and leapt into the sky to grab him.

9

Surya asked Indra, the King of the Gods, for help. 'Stop!' Indra ordered, and threw his special weapon at Hanuman. It hit Hanuman on the jaw and he fell from the sky. He would have fallen to the ground had Vayu, the wind, not caught him.

Vayu was very angry. 'I will take away the breath of all creatures,' he said, and began sucking the air from the universe.

There was panic. Without air there can be no life. The Gods begged Vayu to forgive them and blessed Hanuman with special powers:

'He will be strong and his enemies will fear him. He will be able to move with the speed of lightning. Neither fire nor water will harm him.'

'He will be able to change his size and shape at will.'

'He will live as long as he wants and choose the time of his death.'

Pleased, Vayu released air back into the universe.

Birds, beasts and human beings could breathe again. Vayu added, 'You will be called "Hanuman"—broken jaw. You will be famous for your bravery and loyalty.'

The years went by. Soon it was time for Hanuman to begin his education. Hanuman wanted Surya to be his teacher. 'You see everything. You know everything. Please be my guru.'

Surya replied, 'From morning to evening I ride across the sky. You will have to find another guru.'

Hanuman pleaded, 'I will fly across the sky with you.'

Finally, Surya agreed.

After Hanuman had learnt everything he needed to know, he said to Surya, 'How can I show my gratitude to you?'

What did Hanuman learn?

Surya said, 'Look after my son Sugreev.' Who was Sugreev?

Sugreev was a monkey prince. He had been driven out of his kingdom by his elder brother Bali, and had made his home on a small hill with a few monkey friends. Hanuman met Sugreev and became his adviser.

One day, Sugreev and Hanuman saw a terrifying-looking demon riding in a golden chariot in the sky with a beautiful woman. The woman was crying. As they flew by, she took off some necklaces and bangles and threw them down.

A few days later, Hanuman saw two young men coming towards their hill. Sugreev lived in fear that Bali, who was stronger than him, would attack him. He said to Hanuman, 'Find out who they are. Have they been sent by Bali?'

Hanuman, who could change his shape and size, took the form of a sadhu. 'Who are you?' he asked the visitors.

'I am Ram, Prince of Ayodhya. This is my brother Lakshman. We are looking for my wife Sita.' And he told Hanuman their story.

Ram told Hanuman how he had been sent to the forest for fourteen years and had been living there like a sadhu with his wife and brother. He told Hanuman how the wicked demon Ravan had tricked them and carried Sita away. Searching for Sita, they had come across the dying Jatayu, King of Vultures, who told them his story.

Jatayu had tried to stop Ravan, but Ravan cut off his wings and he fell to the ground. Jatayu also told them that Ravan had taken Sita towards the south.

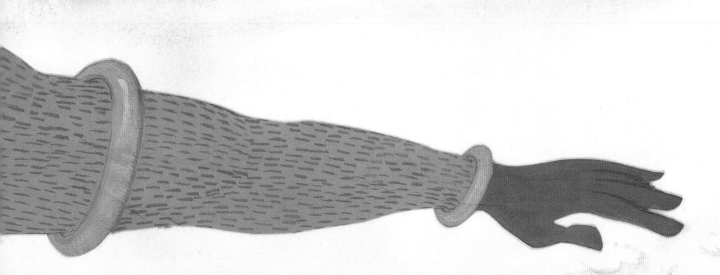

Hanuman in turn told them about Sugreev, and how he was looking for help to defeat Bali and get his kingdom back.

Hanuman realized that Ram and Sugreev could be of great help to one another. Hanuman shed his sadhu form and began to grow. He grew bigger...and...**bigger** and still **bigger**. Carrying Ram and Lakshman on his back, Hanuman flew back to Sugreev.

Sugreev showed Ram the jewels Sita had thrown down. Ram recognized them at once.

Sugreev promised to help Ram find Sita and Ram promised to help Sugreev defeat Bali.

Sugreev challenged Bali to a fight. Ram hid behind some trees, waiting for a chance to help Sugreev and kill Bali. But Sugreev and Bali looked so alike that Ram could not tell which of them was Sugreev and which was Bali. Bali defeated Sugreev.

Hanuman suggested that Sugreev fight Bali again, but this time he should wear a garland of flowers so that Ram could tell them apart.

Sugreev fought Bali again. Ram shot an arrow, which killed Bali.

Find 5 differences between Sugreev and Bali.

23

Now it was Sugreev's turn to help Ram. Urged by Hanuman, Sugreev sent his army of monkeys and bears to look everywhere for Sita, but both he and Ram felt that only Hanuman would be successful in finding Sita.

Ram gave Hanuman his ring. 'Give Sita my ring. She will know you have come from me.'

Searching for Sita, Hanuman and his party of monkeys and bears travelled further and further south till they finally reached the seashore. Here Sampati, Jatayu's elder brother, told them that he had seen Ravan carrying away a beautiful woman across the sea, far away to Lanka. The woman must have been Sita.

ow, only Hanuman could jump far enough to cross the sea to Lanka. Hanuman began to grow in size…big…bigger…and still bigger. Then taking a mighty leap, he flew with the speed of an arrow across the sea.

The sea swarmed with sharks and crocodiles, whales and great fish and water serpents with many coils.

On the way Hanuman had to face many difficulties and dangers. A mountain rose up from the sea and blocked his path. Hanuman knocked the mountain over and flew on towards Lanka.

Then a huge sea monster, Surasa, opened her mouth to swallow him. Hanuman suddenly made himself small…smaller…and still smaller till he was the size of a thumb. He flew into Surasa's mouth and out again in a flash.

Finally, there was a demon who tried to pull him down by his shadow and eat him. Hanuman entered her mouth, tore his way through her body with his sharp nails and came out unhurt.

Find a way out of Surasa's mouth with Hanuman.

29

It was dark when at last Hanuman entered Lanka. He made himself small and began looking for Sita. He peeped into every room of every house, big and small, but there was no sign of her. He searched everywhere, every garden. Where was she?

In how many pictures can you spot Hanuman?

How many trees can you name?

Finally, he saw a beautiful, sad-looking woman in the Ashok Garden, guarded by fierce-looking demons. At last he had found Sita.

Hanuman hid behind a tree and, spotting his chance, dropped Ram's ring in front of Sita. She looked up. Hanuman said, 'I am Hanuman, Ram's messenger. Ram, Lakshman, Sugreev and a large army of monkeys and bears will be here soon to rescue you.'

Sita then gave Hanuman the jewel from her hair to give to Ram.

Before leaving Lanka, Hanuman decided to show Ravan and the demons how strong he was. Hanuman began to grow in size. He grew bigger...and **bigger**...and **bigger**. He pulled up trees and plants by their roots, and threw huge stones at the demons.

Angry, Ravan sent Indrajit, his eldest son, to capture Hanuman. Indrajit shot a very powerful weapon at Hanuman. Hanuman fell down. The demons tied him up and took him to Ravan.

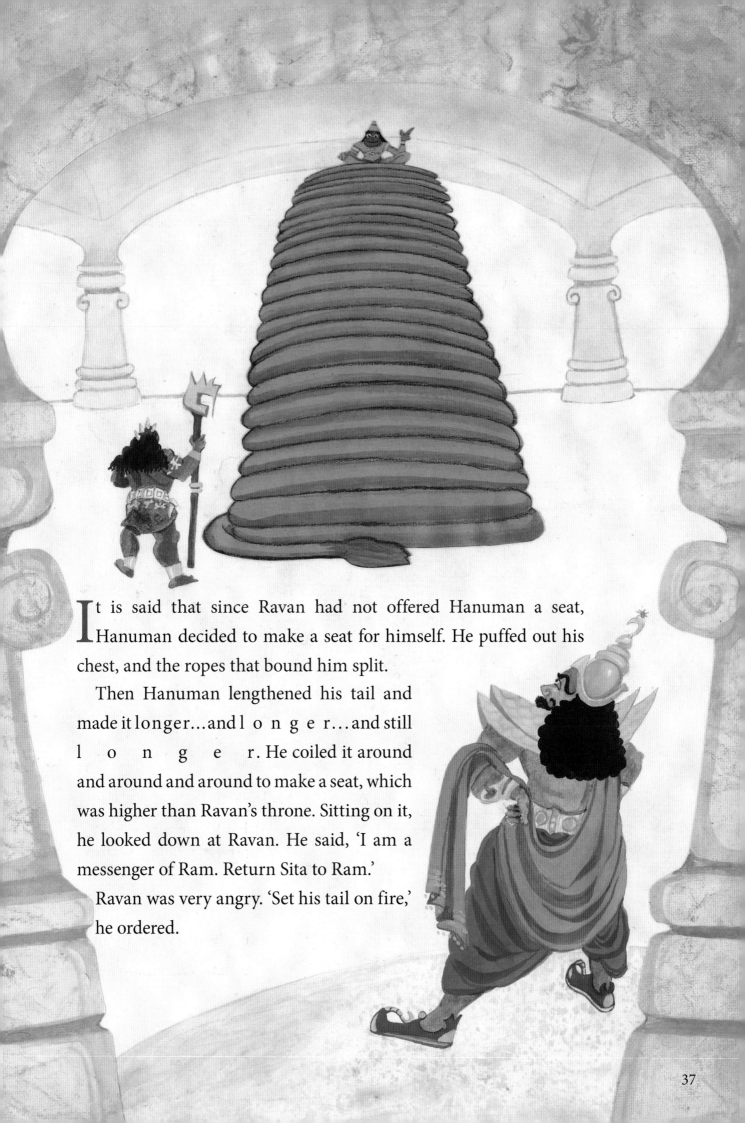

It is said that since Ravan had not offered Hanuman a seat, Hanuman decided to make a seat for himself. He puffed out his chest, and the ropes that bound him split.

Then Hanuman lengthened his tail and made it l o n g e r…and l o n g e r…and still l o n g e r. He coiled it around and around and around to make a seat, which was higher than Ravan's throne. Sitting on it, he looked down at Ravan. He said, 'I am a messenger of Ram. Return Sita to Ram.'

Ravan was very angry. 'Set his tail on fire,' he ordered.

The demons held him and began to wrap oil-soaked cotton strips around Hanuman's tail. But as they did so, Hanuman's tail began to grow—l o n g e r...and l o n g e r. When they were finally able to cover the tail, they set fire to it.

But Hanuman had been blessed that fire would not harm him. Once again he increased his size. He grew bigger...and bigger... and still bigger. And, jumping from rooftop to rooftop, Hanuman swung his tail and set fire to the city.

Find your way to the island of Lanka with Hanuman.

Then Hanuman flew back with the speed of lightning. He gave Ram Sita's jewel. Ram hugged Hanuman. 'No one else could have done what you have done,' said Ram.

Ram, Lakshman, Sugreev and the army of monkeys and bears set off for Lanka, determined to destroy the ten-headed Ravan and his demons.

They reached the seashore, but how were they going to cross the ocean to reach Lanka?

Finally, it was decided to build a bridge under the sharp eye of Hanuman. The army of monkeys and bears pulled out big trees and rolled down large rocks to the shore to make the bridge. Hanuman carved the name 'Ram' with his nails on the rocks.

How many rocks with 'Ram' written on them can you count?

When the bridge was ready, thousands of monkeys and bears began crossing over to Lanka. It is said that just then Ravan threw a weapon, which broke the end of the bridge. Ram and his army were caught midway—they could not cross over to Lanka.

Hanuman once again increased his size. He stretched himself and covered the gap—his hands on the shore of Lanka, his feet touching the edge of the bridge. Thus, climbing over him, the army crossed over to Lanka.

The battle began. Hanuman carried Ram on his shoulders. It was a fierce battle. The demons attacked with spears and clubs. The monkeys fought with their teeth and nails, with trees they uprooted and with rocks. Thousands were killed.

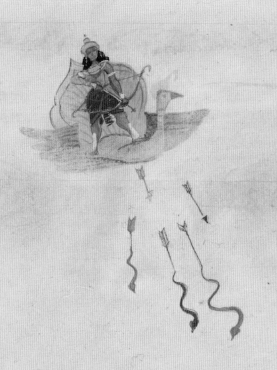

During the battle, Indrajit, Ravan's son, shot at Ram and Lakshman with arrows that turned into snakes. The snakes coiled themselves around Ram and Lakshman, and the two princes could not move.

Suddenly the eagle, Garuda, King of the Birds, arrived. As soon as the snakes saw Garuda, they fled. Because eagles kill and eat snakes.

The battle continued. Soldiers on both sides, monkeys and demons, were killed.

Finally, Ravan ordered that his brother, Kumbhkaran, should be woken up. Kumbhkaran was a giant, the mightiest of the demons. He slept for six months of the year and was very hungry when he woke up. So, Ravan had mountains of food ready for him.

To wake Kumbhkaran, trumpets were blown into his ears, drums and gongs were beaten, buckets of water poured on his face. Finally, they drove horses, camels and a thousand elephants over his body.

At last, Kumbhkaran awoke. After he had eaten his fill, Kumbhkaran went into battle. At the sight of this giant, who was as huge as a mountain, the monkeys ran away in terror. But Hanuman placed himself in Kumbhkaran's path and attacked him with a mountain peak. And when Kumbhkaran threw his spear at Sugreev, Hanuman caught it and broke it across his knee. Encouraged, thousands of monkeys rushed at Kumbhkaran, climbed up his body, and bit and scratched him.

Meanwhile, Ram attacked Kumbhkaran with more and more powerful arrows. First Kumbhkaran's arms were cut off, then his legs. But he kept moving forward, fighting. Then, with an even more powerful arrow, Kumbhkaran's head was cut off.

Finally, Ravan himself entered the battle. He hurled a spear, bright as the sun, at Lakshman. The spear pierced Lakshman's chest and Lakshman fell to the ground.

Ram's eyes filled with tears. 'I love my brother more than life itself. Why should I live now?' he cried. But Ram was told that a special herb, the sanjivini, which grew far away on the Mountain of Herbs in the Himalayas, could revive Lakshman.

Find the sanjivini herb.

So Hanuman once again increased his size, and flew to the Mountain of Herbs. But, when he got there, he could not recognize the sanjivini herb. 'I will take back the entire mountain,' Hanuman said and lifting the entire mountain, he flew back to the battlefield.

Breathing in a paste of the sanjivini herb, Lakshman immediately recovered.

Now it was time for the final battle between Ram and the ten-headed demon king Ravan. Ram's arrows whizzed like lightning and pierced Ravan's ten heads, one by one. But as one head fell, another grew in its place. Ram and Ravan fought fiercely for seven days and seven nights. Finally, Ram used a special weapon. It flew through the air, throwing out flames, struck Ravan in the chest and killed him.

Ram asked Hanuman to fly to Lanka and tell Sita of Ravan's death. Sita went to meet Ram, and the army of monkeys and bears who had fought so bravely to rescue her.

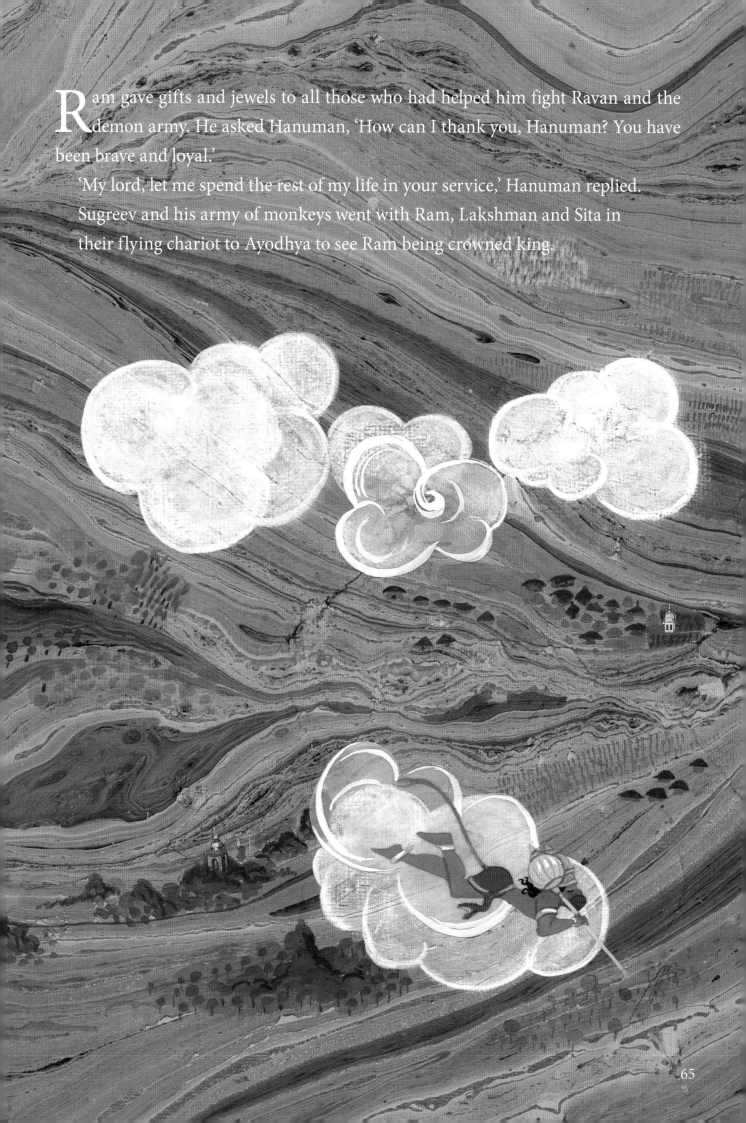

Ram gave gifts and jewels to all those who had helped him fight Ravan and the demon army. He asked Hanuman, 'How can I thank you, Hanuman? You have been brave and loyal.'

'My lord, let me spend the rest of my life in your service,' Hanuman replied.

Sugreev and his army of monkeys went with Ram, Lakshman and Sita in their flying chariot to Ayodhya to see Ram being crowned king.

R am was crowned king. He gave clothes and jewels to Hanuman. Sita took off her own necklace of pearls and gave it to Hanuman.

I t is said that one day Hanuman broke the necklace and looked carefully at each pearl.

'What are you looking for?' asked the people.

'I am looking for Ram and Sita,' Hanuman replied.

'They are sitting on the throne.'

'They are in all things. They are in my heart. I am looking for them in these pearls.'

'Ram and Sita are in your heart? Show them to us.'

Hanuman immediately tore open his chest with his nails. There, on his heart, was the image of Ram and Sita.

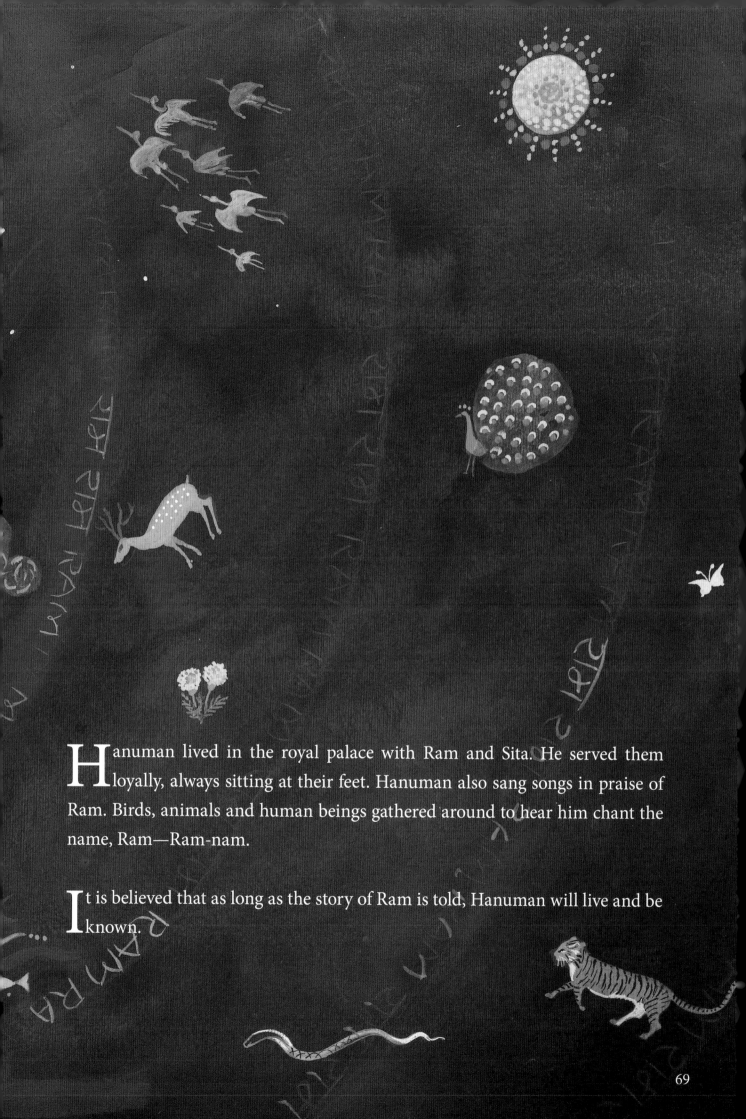

Hanuman lived in the royal palace with Ram and Sita. He served them loyally, always sitting at their feet. Hanuman also sang songs in praise of Ram. Birds, animals and human beings gathered around to hear him chant the name, Ram—Ram-nam.

It is believed that as long as the story of Ram is told, Hanuman will live and be known.

Over the years many stories began to be told of Hanuman's strength. It is said that Bhim, the mighty Pandav, once came upon an old monkey sitting across the road. 'Get up. Let me pass,' Bhim ordered.

'I am old and ill. Move my tail aside and go past,' Hanuman replied.

Bhim tried to push the tail aside. First, he used one hand, and when he could not move the tail, he used both hands. But even then he could not move the tail an inch. 'You are no ordinary monkey,' Bhim said. 'Who are you?'

'I am Hanuman,' the monkey replied.

Bhim fell at his feet and begged Hanuman to forgive him.

Page 14-15:

Music

Dance

Fighting

Study

Medicine

Page 22-23: 5 differences

Page 32-33:

Page 34-35:

Banana

Ashoka

Pomegranate

Hibiscus

Mango

Plumeria
(Champa)

Page 58-59:

Page 43: More than 12 rocks